As the crow flies series

Joe the Crow Explores Wisconsin

Copyright © 2024
Barbara Morris

All rights reserved.
No part of this publication may be reproduced, stored in a retrieval system, or transmitted in any form or by any means, electronic, mechanical, photocopying, recording (including but not limited to storytime videos), or otherwise, without written permission from the publisher. For information regarding permission, write to Barbara Morris.

Published in Mebane, North Carolina

Paperback ISBN:
978-1-957880-09-9

Joe the Crow Explores Wisconsin

Dedication

To Jesus Christ, through whom all things are possible.

To my husband, Ron, who supported me through the process so I could make my dream come true.

To Riley, who inspires me by demonstrating passion and determination for the things he enjoys.

To Nikki and her husband Hayden, who taught me to have enough faith to jump in and just do it!

To Craig for his proofreading skills.

Thanks to Beth Brigham and my brother Randy for sharing all your Wisconsin knowledge

Meet Joe the Crow

Can you help Joe the Crow find the following?

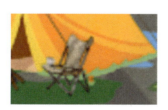

Joe woke up bright and early and went in search of breakfast. He found a yummy treat of corn from a nearby bird feeder.

After filling his tummy, he continued his journey of exploring the world.

Joe landed on a big red barn and spied several cows. He had seen cows when he visited Iowa, but these cows seemed different. They each took a turn going into the barn.

Joe decided to investigate what was happening in the barn.

Joe flew through the door and landed on a milk can. He heard a funny sound. Something attached to the cow's utter made a "swish, swish, swish" sound. Joe could see a white liquid being pumped by the machine. He realized this was how milk was made.

Joe flew out of the barn just as a big milk truck left the farm. He decided to follow the truck and see where it delivered the milk.

Welcome to the Cheese Factory

The truck drove into a building, and Joe lost sight of it. He noticed a window was open and landed on the ledge. He saw two men stirring a big container of milk.

He realized that they were using the milk from the truck to make the big wheels of cheese he saw on the shelves.

Welcome to Wisconsin Dells!

Visit
Paul Bunyan's Cook Shanty
Restaurant

Joe continued his journey and flew by a huge sign welcoming him to Wisconsin Dells. He was unsure what lay ahead, but based on the size of the sign, it must be a big deal!

Joe heard laughter and squealing as he flew over the water park packed with kids. It was a warm day, so swimming in the fabulous pool and slipping down the giant slide must have felt good.

Joe smelled something funny as he flew over the go-cart track. The little cars sputtered as they flew around the track, and the kids squealed with delight as they slid around the twisting turns!

Joe came upon an odd scene. He noticed that the side of the bus said, "Wisconsin Dells Duck Rides." Joe was amazed that a bus was called a duck and could drive on the road and float in the water.

As Joe flew along the river, he came across a big boat. He heard music playing and smelled yummy food. He thought he might enjoy such a ride if he weren't so busy sightseeing.

Joe flew back over dry land and headed toward Milwaukee. He wondered what wonders he would see in this town.

Welcome to Milwaukee

Harley Davidson Motorcycle founded in 1903

The cars were heading toward a football stadium. Joe heard cheering and a man's voice blaring over a loud speaker. He decided to fly in for a closer look.

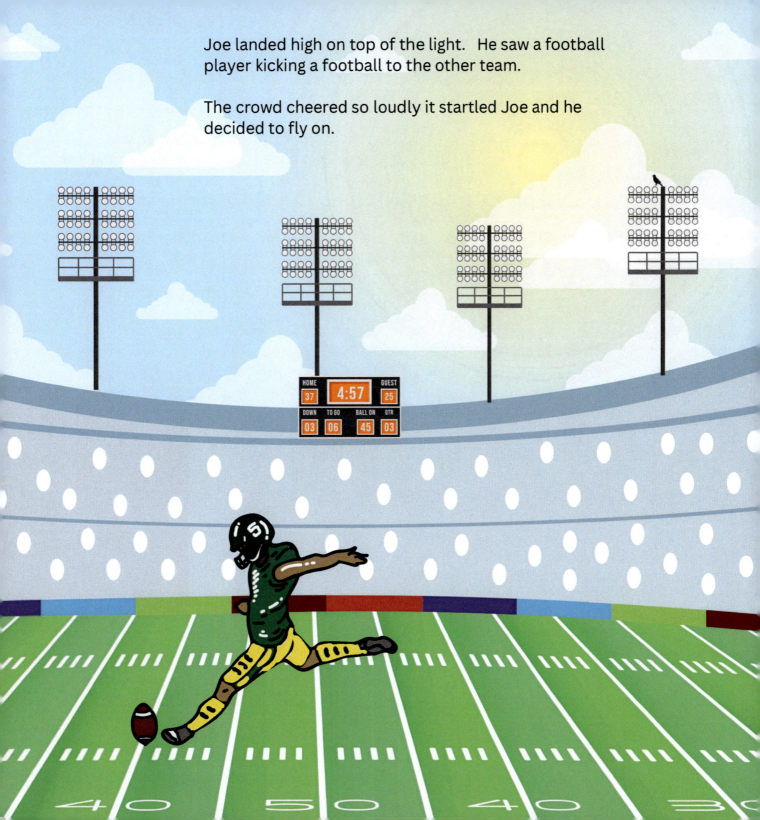

Joe landed high on top of the light. He saw a football player kicking a football to the other team.

The crowd cheered so loudly it startled Joe and he decided to fly on.

Joe flew by a beautiful sugar maple tree shading a family of robins on his way to see Lake Superior.

Fun Fact from Joe: The sugar maple is Wisconsin's state tree, and the American robin is its state bird.

Joe settled on a rock beside Lake Superior and watched the butterflies float in the warm breeze. Joe inhaled the wonderful smell of the sweet violet, Wisconsin's state flower.

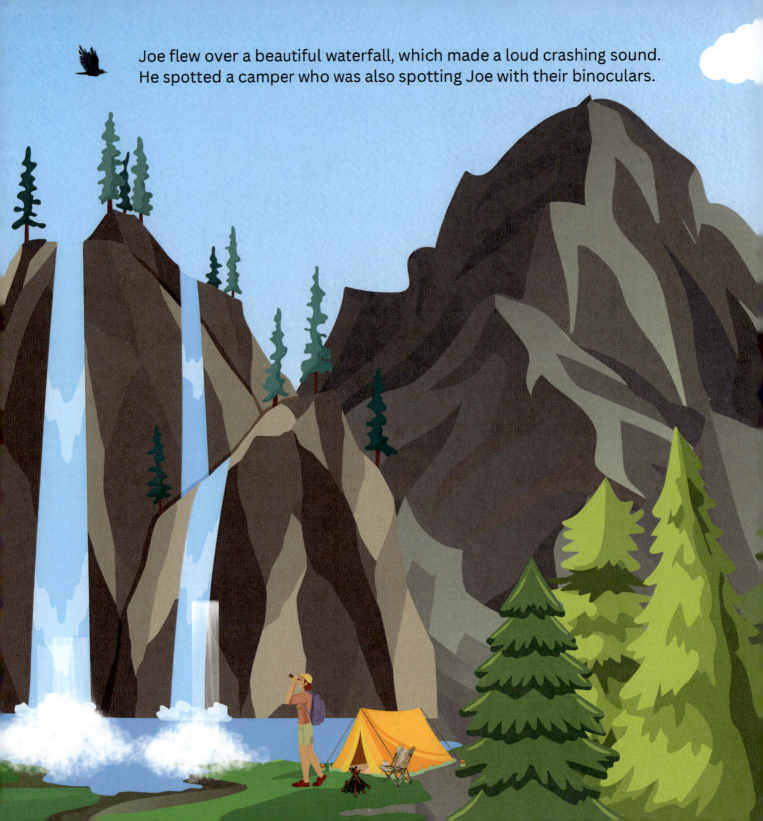
Joe flew over a beautiful waterfall, which made a loud crashing sound. He spotted a camper who was also spotting Joe with their binoculars.

Joe flew for quite a while before coming to a sign for Door County. Joe wondered what marvelous sites lie ahead.

Joe was excited to see the beautiful lighthouse sitting on the shore. Its light was so bright that he had to look away.

After a while, it started to get dark, and Joe decided to rest for the night. He noticed a boat below and decided to follow it in the morning. But for now, Joe will close his eyes and get some much-needed sleep.

About the Author

Barbara Morris had a lifelong dream of publishing a children's book series. In 2021, she pursued her dream and self-published her first of six books in the series, "The Adventures of Nikki and Abbey Dog".

Some adventures in the series are based on events that occurred during her childhood or with her children.

In 2023, she began her second series of books which feature "Joe the Crow", who travels from state to state seeing all the sites.

The series is both educational and has a search and find component.

More titles from the series:

"As the Crow flies"

Available now on Amazon:

Book 1:
Joe the Crow Explores Iowa

Check out another series by the author:

"The Adventures of Nikki and Abbey Dog"

Available now on Amazon

Stay tuned for Joe's next adventure……

Made in the USA
Middletown, DE
14 October 2024